Raintree is an imprint of Capstone Global Library Limited, a company incorporated in
England and Wales having its registered office at 7 Pilgrim Street, London, EC4V 6LB –
Registered company number: 6695582

www.raintree.co.uk
myorders@raintree.co.uk

Printed and bound in China.

ISBN 978-1-4062-9410-1
18 17 16 15 14
10 9 8 7 6 5 4 3 2 1

British Library Cataloguing in Publication Data
A full catalogue record for this book is available from the British Library.

Cover art and illustrations by Lisa K. Weber
Design: K. Carlson
Editorial: A. Deering
Production: G. Bentdahl

Acknowledgements: Shutterstock (vector images, backgrounds, paper textures)

The Case of the
STOLEN SCULPTURE

By Steve Brezenoff
Illustrated by Lisa K. Weber

raintree
a Capstone company — publishers for children

The Statues of Gudea

- Twenty-seven statues discovered so far

- Statues depict Gudea, a ruler of Lagash in Southern Mesopotamia, who reigned for at least 11 years

- General features: cylindrical form, muscular arms, clasped hands, enlarged eyes

- Statues were designed to represent Gudea in temples so subjects could pray and make offerings

- Each statue bears a unique inscription

- Early statues were small and made of local stones such as limestone, steatite and alabaster

- Later statues were made of more expensive materials, such as diorite

Amal Farah

Raining Sam

Wilson Kipper

Clementine Wim

Capitol City Sleuths

Amal Farah
Age: 11
Favourite Museum: Air and Space Museum
Interests: astronomy, space travel and
building models of spaceships

Raining Sam
Age: 12
Favourite Museum: American History Museum
Interests: Ojibwe history, culture and
traditions, American history – good and bad

Clementine Wim
Age: 13
Favourite Museum: Museum of Art
Interests: painting, sculpting with clay and
anything colourful

Wilson Kipper
Age: 10
Favourite Museum: Natural History Museum
Interests: dinosaurs (especially pterosaurs
and herbivores) and building dinosaur models

TABLE OF

CONTENTS

CHAPTER 1
Stolen!

Thirteen-year-old Clementine Wim woke up just as the sun was rising, which was a little unusual for her. She normally preferred to lie in, but today she was on a mission. She grabbed her drink off the kitchen table – hers was the orange juice – and hurried out of the house, not even bothering to put her shoes on.

Pulling open the door, Clementine stepped inside the garage. At least, it was supposed to be a garage. But with the old charity-shop sofas and rainbow rug on the floor, plus the painting easel and pottery wheel, it was more like an art studio than anything else. Which was just the way Clementine liked it.

Heading straight to the easel, Clementine studied the painting she'd left unfinished at bedtime the night before. So far it was a field of red, which gradually shifted to a field of green across the huge canvas. She thought maybe it represented something – she just wasn't sure what. But she did know she wanted to get the colours exactly right, and she was having trouble.

Clementine poked at the green with a little bit of cobalt blue on her brush. The

moment the bristles of her brush touched the canvas, her phone rang. She flinched, and sent a smear of blue paint across the canvas.

"Oh no!" Clementine shrieked, stomping one foot. She threw down her brush and grabbed the phone. "Hello!"

"Um, hi?" said Amal Farah, one of her best friends. "Is everything okay?"

Clementine sighed. "Yes, I was just…" She stared at the painting, with its field of red and of green now accented by the startling blue streak across the middle, and smiled. "Actually, yes. Everything is okay. In fact it's perfect. I love it. Thank you."

"You're welcome?" Amal replied, sounding confused. "Have you spoken to your mum?"

Clementine had to think about it. She was easily distracted, and it was possible she'd spoken to her mum and completely forgotten about it. "I don't think so," she said. "Why?"

"Because she's on TV," Amal said.

"Is she?" Clementine said. "Why?"

The news was more than a bit surprising. Clementine's mother, an assistant curator at the Capitol City Museum of Art, had certainly never been on TV before. In fact, she didn't even watch TV. They had an old TV tucked away in a corner of the house, but Clementine had never once seen it turned on.

"Hold on," Amal said. "She's on again." Clementine heard the phone bumping around, and then the sound of a news reader introducing Dr Abigail Wim, Clementine's mother.

"It's very upsetting, of course," Dr Wim was saying. "The Statue of Gudea cannot be found. We have to assume it's been stolen. Everyone here at the museum is simply distraught. We appreciate any help the public can offer."

The sound of the news faded away, and Amal came back on the line. "Now they're showing a photo of the statue," she said. "It looks amazing."

Clementine knew the statue very well. She'd seen it many times, and had even sketched it and painted it a few times over the years. Her mother was very proud to have it at the museum's collection. It was worth millions – no one really knew how much.

"Have you called the boys?" Clementine asked. She meant their friends Wilson Kipper and Raining Sam. The four of them did almost everything together – but solving museum mysteries like this one was their favourite thing to do.

"Not yet," Amal said. "I thought I'd speak to you first."

"Thanks," Clementine said. She put her brushes into a cup of cleaner, found her old trainers under the sofa and opened the garage door. "Ask them to meet us at the museum. And hurry!" With that, she climbed onto her old bike and sped away.

Clementine pedalled furiously, but she just couldn't go fast enough. Most of the time she loved her silly old bike. The basket on the front and the three different bells and the big comfy seat and the flag flying behind her left shoulder were fun and funky – perfect for her. But today, for the first time, Clementine wished she had a road bike like Amal's.

"Come on, come on," Clementine muttered through her teeth as she pedalled up the hill at the end of O'Keefe Boulevard.

At the top of the road, on the highest hill in the city, stood the Capitol City Museum of Art. Its front, made of huge panes of glass and curled sheets of gleaming steel, glinted brightly in the mid-morning sunshine.

The sunlight was so bright in fact,

that when it was reflected right into Clementine's eyes, she nearly lost control of the bike. Luckily, she managed to steady her handlebars at the last minute.

Clementine breathed a sigh of relief. She couldn't afford any setbacks. Not with the Statue of Gudea missing. *I have to get to the museum*, she thought. *It's up to us to get it back.*

CHAPTER 2
Silver lining?

When Clementine finally reached the museum, she was in for another surprise. "Wow," she cried. She hadn't seen the entrance hall this crowded since the Picasso exhibition two summers ago. But this was no ordinary crowd of art fans. This was a mob.

Clementine, already tall for a thirteen-year-old, stood up on her toes and called out, "Amal? Are you here?"

Amal's head – instantly recognizable thanks to the star-patterned hijab she always wore – appeared above the crowd. She was standing close to the ticket office and quickly waved Clementine over.

Clementine pushed her way through the mob. "Guys," she gasped when she reached Amal. Raining and Wilson were standing beside her. "What is going *on* here?"

"It's the robbery," Wilson said, keeping his eyes on his tablet computer, which he poked and swiped and squinted at. "It's all over the local news. Your mum is a big star."

"I wonder where she is," Clementine said, looking around the crowded hall.

"We haven't seen her yet," Raining said.

Just then, a man wearing a vibrant blue

suit, a bright shirt, and an orange tie strode towards the entrance hall from the long corridor beyond the ticket office.

"Who's that?" Wilson asked, finally looking up.

"That's Mr Carbony," Clementine told her friends. "He's the head of the education and community relations department."

Mr Carbony climbed up onto the ticket desk and raised his arms. The crowd went quiet, and he coughed and cleared his throat.

"Thank you all for supporting the museum during this difficult time," he said. He pulled an orange handkerchief from his lapel and patted his tearful eyes. "As you must have heard by now on the various news websites covering this story, our Statue of Gudea has been stolen. Thankfully, our insurance company has been most accommodating and helpful during this ordeal."

"He's already contacted the insurance company! Does that mean they're giving up?" Clementine whispered to her friends. "So soon?"

"When the statue was discovered missing yesterday morning," Mr Carbony went on, "our director immediately notified the police and the insurance company. While the police investigation will continue, the insurance company's investigation has been completed and the payment has been approved."

"Wow," Amal whispered, looking surprised. "They're paying out before the police have closed the case?"

Clementine shrugged, keeping her eyes on Mr Carbony. He grinned – despite the tears – and clasped his hands.

"Which brings me to the exciting news," he continued. "Something of a silver lining to the big grey cloud we're faced with here at the Capitol City Museum of Art this week."

"What does he mean 'a silver lining'?" Clementine whispered – a little too loudly. Some of the crowd turned to glare at her. She didn't care. The Statue of Gudea was one of her favourite items in the museum, and Mr Carbony was talking about giving up the search and silver linings! She was so cross!

"As some of you may remember, I recently proposed a new educational wing for the museum," Mr Carbony continued. "Unfortunately, the board could not approve the new wing due to a lack of funds. But thanks to the very generous insurance policy the museum held for our Gudea, I am now pleased to announce that the new wing will be possible after all!"

The crowd seemed to gasp collectively for just an instant. Then they erupted with applause.

"Thank you, thank you," Mr Carbony said. "Now, the insurance payment is a good sum, but even with that money, we still won't be able to include all the wonderful features we had in mind. But regardless, it will be a great resource for the community and, in particular, for the children of Capitol City."

The applause surged again. Clementine took Wilson by the hand and pulled him out of the crowd, nodding for Amal and Raining to join them. They gathered near the entrance to the Greats of American Painting exhibition, where the roar of the crowd and Mr Carbony's endless speech weren't so loud.

"I suppose that *is* a silver lining," Amal said. She looked at Clementine. "You've been hoping they'd find the money to build that wing, haven't you?"

"I have, but..." Clementine trailed off. She had to admit, the new wing *was* good news. Still, the idea that the Gudea was gone and no one was looking for it made her absolutely miserable. She tried to smile, but her grin flopped.

"Don't cry, Clemmy," said Wilson, putting a comforting arm around her shoulders.

Clementine knew Wilson was just trying to make her feel better, so she forgave him for calling her "Clemmy". But given that she was one and a half feet taller than Wilson, his arm around her shoulders was a bit awkward.

"I'm not crying," she said, sniffling, but she could have been. Clementine cried a little more easily than she would have liked. "We should find my mum."

* * *

"I'm telling you, Mr Carbony," said Dr Wim a few moments later. "The phone has been ringing non-stop!"

Clementine and her friends stepped into her mum's office and huddled together near the door. The office was small and cramped with papers, boxes, crates and poster tubes. Books, books and more books were piled on every surface and on most of the floor.

Dr Wim flashed the children a grin and moved the phone from one ear to the other. "Everyone wants to help out," she went on, talking into the phone. "One of our members is organizing an event to help raise additional funds ... all right ... bye."

Clementine's mother hung up the phone and turned to face them. "Clementine!" she said, pulling off her glasses and sticking them into the thick bun of greying blonde hair on top of her head. "What are you doing here?"

"I heard about the Gudea," Clementine said. "I'm so upset."

"Oh, sweetheart," her mum said with a sympathetic smile.

"I thought you would be too," Clementine went on.

Dr Wim frowned at her. She stepped around the clutter on the floor and bent down in front of Clementine, putting a hand on each shoulder. "Actually," she said, "I was distraught. But then Mr Carbony and I realized how much *good* this insurance money could do for the museum and for the community."

"I suppose so," Clementine admitted.

Dr Wim patted her shoulders and straightened up.

"What were you and Mr Carbony talking about just now?" Raining asked.

"Hm?" said Dr Wim.

"On the phone," Raining explained.

"Raining," Amal said. "That's none of your business. I'm sure it's just museum-business."

"Oh, it's fine," Dr Wim said. She went to her desk and poked around among the stacks of paper and notebooks. Then she lifted up her computer's keyboard and peeked underneath. "I was just telling him that since his announcement – in just the past thirty minutes – the museum's members have banded together. They're going to raise even *more* money so all of our dreams for the new education wing can come true. Isn't that *marvellous*?"

"Yes, Mum," said Clementine. She managed to force a smile this time. "That's great."

"Um, Dr Wim?" Amal said, stepping up to the desk. "Are you looking for something?"

"I swear," said Dr Wim, "if I had a penny for every pair of glasses I lose in this silly office..."

Amal reached up and pulled the glasses out of Dr Wim's hair, where she'd stuck them moments earlier. "These glasses?" she said.

"Oh, thank you!" Dr Wim said. She slipped them on. "Where did you find them?"

CHAPTER 3
On the case

"Thanks for coming to the museum," Clementine said as the four friends walked down the back corridor, where all the offices were located, towards the main part of the museum. "But I don't think we'll be solving any mysteries this time."

"Why not?" Raining asked.

"Haven't you noticed? Everyone here seems *happy* the Gudea is gone," Clementine said with a little shrug.

"Maybe I should just forget about it. I can spend the day going door-to-door to raise more money for the new wing."

Amal glanced at her doubtfully. "Is that what you really want?" she asked. "If it is, we'll forget about the statue. I'll even help you raise some money."

"Yeah," Raining agreed. "A cute kid like me could bring in some serious cash."

Clementine laughed. "Oh, you know that's not what I want!" she said, smiling. "I want to find the Gudea."

"Good," said Amal. "I don't feel like walking all over the city knocking on doors today anyway. It's far too hot outside."

"Now that that's settled," Wilson said, "I think I know where we should start."

* * *

Moments later, Amal strode right up to Mr Carbony's office, her three best friends at her heels, and knocked three times – *thump thump thump* – on the door.

"Yes?" a voice answered from inside.

Amal pushed open the door, and they all stepped into Mr Carbony's office. His office, just like Dr Wim's, was a mess of clutter. But while Dr Wim's office was mostly papers and books, Mr Carbony's was full of stacks and stacks of crates and boxes.

"Can I help – oh, Clementine Wim," Mr Carbony said. "How are you?"

"I'm fine, Mr Carbony," said Clementine. "These are my friends."

Mr Carbony nodded at the others. "Are you all looking forwards to next autumn, when our new education wing is expected to be completed?"

"How do you already know when the wing will be finished?" Clementine asked. "I'm still reeling from the theft!"

"Oh, you can be very sure that we're all still smarting from that," Mr Carbony said. He walked around his desk and sat on the edge facing them. He put his hands over his chest and frowned. "But though our hearts are breaking, we feel reassured that the hearts of our *children* will grow ten times when they see the new wing we are building *just for them*."

"So ... the statue went missing yesterday?" Wilson asked. He clicked on his tablet, ready to take notes.

"Well, no," said Mr Carbony. "It was last seen on Saturday at closing time. A little after seven that evening, I believe. When we opened on Tuesday morning, it was gone."

"So it could have been stolen at any point over the weekend," Amal pointed out. Several of the Capitol City museums, including The Museum of Art, were closed on Sundays and Mondays.

"Except that no one can get into the museum at the weekend," Carbony said.

"No one?" said Raining. "But what about – oh, I don't know – you?"

"*Moi?*" Mr Carbony said, clearly very taken aback. "What are you implying?"

Clementine jumped between Mr Carbony and Raining. "He just means that some of the staff must have keys," she said quickly. "So maybe someone with a key came in over the weekend."

"No, no, no," Mr Carbony said, shaking his head. "Entering the museum is not like unlocking the front door of your house and strolling in. There's a key to the steel gate, another for the glass doors and revolving door, and an electronic security panel with a twelve-digit code and fingerprint-matching system."

"So if someone typed in their code," Wilson said, "or scanned their fingerprints, the information would save onto the security computer."

"Naturally," said Mr Carbony. The phone on his desk rang – a series of three loud chirps – and he walked back around to the other side of his desk to answer it.

"And has someone checked the security computer?" Amal asked.

Mr Carbony lifted the receiver and covered the mouthpiece. "Well, I assume so," he said. "There was an investigation, after all. They even searched *my house.*" He put the phone to his ear and signalled for the children to leave. "This is Mr Carbony ... oh, *hello*, Mrs Claypool."

Clementine ushered her friends out of the door and closed it behind them. "To the security office?" she asked.

"Of course," Raining replied. "But I'll admit, I'm stumped."

"Already?" Clementine asked.

Wilson nodded. "Me too," he agreed. "I thought this was Mr Carbony's work, but he was so quick to point us to the security computer. I doubt he'd do that if he knew it was going to implicate him. Plus they searched his house."

"Well, we might as well check," Amal said. "If the computer is really keeping a log, and Mr Carbony came in over the weekend, it'll prove he did it."

CHAPTER 4
Security

A few moments later, they were at the security office. Clementine knocked lightly and walked in.

"Hi, Clementine," said Judy, the security guard on duty. She swivelled around in her chair, which faced a bank of monitors showing all of the different rooms in the museum. Each monitor's image changed every few seconds. From Judy's chair, you

could see nearly every square centimetre of the museum in just a few minutes.

"Hi, Judy," Clementine replied, sitting down in the only extra chair. She noted the guard's serious-looking expression. "What's wrong? You don't seem very happy."

"I'm not," Judy said, shaking her head. "How do you think a theft like this makes us look? Everyone on the security team is taking this really badly."

"Mr Carbony told us how difficult it is to get into this place when it's closed," Amal said.

Judy nodded. "He's right. There are several precautions in place to prevent intruders from getting inside – a steel gate, several sets of doors, a security panel and a fingerprint system. And even if someone was able to get inside, there are motion-activated security cameras located throughout the museum."

"So the cameras would capture anyone inside? Even employees?" Wilson asked.

Judy nodded again. "Everyone," she said. "The president of the Association of Capitol City Museums could come in – with his key and his personal security code and his very own fingerprints – and as soon as he stepped into the entrance hall, the cameras would start recording his every move."

"So," Clementine said, looking warily around the little security office, "are there cameras recording us right now?"

"Yes, even in here," Judy said. She

pointed one long, well-manicured finger at the darkest corner of the ceiling, where a tiny red light flashed slowly.

When Clementine squinted, she could just make out the camera's shining black lens.

"And before you ask, yes. The security team – including me – went through every second of security footage from the past few days," Judy continued. "No one was in this museum between closing time on Saturday and opening time on Tuesday morning."

"No one at all?" Amal asked.

"No one," said Judy. "Unless they came in through the roof – and were invisible and weightless."

* * *

"Now what?" Raining said as the four friends walked slowly through the Greek and Roman Sculpture Hall.

"Were you here at all on Tuesday morning, Clemmy?" Wilson asked.

Clementine thought about it for a minute. She often had a hard time remembering what happened on what day.

"Um, on Tuesday..." she said. In her mind, she went back over the days, thinking about what she'd done. Over the past few days, she'd started her red-green painting, thrown two pots on the wheel and tried to make a stained glass Christmas tree ornament for the fourth time. She could never get the soldering part quite right.

"Oh!" Clementine exclaimed as she suddenly remembered. "I *was* here on Tuesday morning. I came down with my mum, and we went in at opening time – before, actually. I was already in the Hopper gallery at nine when the museum officially opened."

"The Hopper gallery?" Amal repeated. "Is that where that frog sculpture is?"

Clementine laughed. "No," she said. "*Edward* Hopper, the painter. An exhibition of his work is on loan here this year."

"And you didn't hear anything about the stolen statue until the next morning?" Wilson asked.

Clementine shrugged one shoulder. "I was busy," she said. "You know I like to draw copies of my favourite pieces. I had my colouring pencils with me on Tuesday, and I spent the whole morning sketching *The House by the Railroad*."

"Well," Amal said, "did you notice anything that morning?"

Clementine tried hard to think, but all she could remember was Hopper's painting of the big old scary-looking house next to the train tracks and her own inadequate pencil copy.

"Let's go to the Hopper exhibition," Raining suggested. "Maybe it'll jog your memory."

"It's worth a try," Clementine said, and she led the way.

CHAPTER 5
Retracing

The friends walked through the
museum – a building on three floors with
all sorts of exhibitions piled upon each
other. They passed through the Chinese
Figure Painting exhibition, the Persian
Pottery Hall, the third-floor Tea Room and
Amal's favourite, the Hall of Glass Art.
The pieces in there – most of them small
enough to fit into the palm of your hand –
glittered like jewels in the sunlight.

"The Hopper exhibition is in the next room," Clementine said, passing through the sunlit room of glass pieces and into a darker chamber beyond. In there, the paintings were lit with spotlights.

"I sat there," Clementine said, pointing to a pair of wooden benches in the centre of the room. She walked over and sat down, facing a painting labelled *The House by the Railroad*. Her friends trailed after her.

"How long did you sit here?" Wilson asked. "All morning?"

Clementine nodded. "Yes, up until lunchtime," she said. "I – no, wait a minute. I got a cup of tea. I had to clear my head and think about Hopper's use of light and shadow." She shook her head mournfully. "It was so hard to duplicate with my pencils. I mean, it would have been hard with paint, too, I suppose."

"Stay on track, Clementine," Amal said. "Let's retrace your steps to the Tea Room."

Everyone followed Clementine back through the Hall of Glass Art and into the Persian Pottery Hall. She immediately turned left and stepped into a little sunlit café. The Tea Room boasted five small tables and ten chairs. A pair of miniature trees, perfectly pruned so they looked like lollipops, flanked the counter at the back.

"Hi, everyone," said Alyssa, the woman working at the café. "Cup of tea, Clementine? Or a flapjack today? They're just out of the oven and still warm."

"Ooh," said Clementine, taking a step towards the counter.

Wilson grabbed her. "No snacks," he said. "We're working, remember?"

"Fine," Clementine said. "Alyssa, you were here when I came in yesterday. Do you remember anything strange happening?"

Alyssa shook her head. "No, it was a normal day," she said. "I saw you at about ten o'clock. You and that woman who was already here when you came in. You were my only customers until lunchtime."

"Woman?" Amal said. "What woman?"

Alyssa shrugged. "I don't think it was anyone important. Just a woman."

Raining turned to Clementine. "Do you remember her?" he asked.

"Let me think," Clementine said. "I walked in, and I had my eyes on my drawing. I couldn't stop thinking about the windows on the left-hand side of the house. They look like tired, crazy eyes. It's really very – "

"Stay on track, Clemmy," Wilson said.

"Oh, okay," Clementine said. "Well, my eyes were on the paper, so I bumped into someone. I said excuse me, but she got very irritated."

"Yes," Alyssa said, nodding. "That was her. I'd forgotten about that. She almost dropped her package."

"Did she?" Clementine asked.

"Yes," Alyssa said. "She'd been telling me about it just before you came in. She said she bought it down in the gift shop as a gift for her son. Very fragile."

"How big was it?" Amal asked.

Alyssa used her hands to map out the size of a box approximately 30-centimetres wide and 60-centimetres high.

"Hmm," Amal said. "The Statue of Gudea was here on the third floor, wasn't it?"

"Yes," Clementine confirmed. "In the Mesopotamian collection."

"And the gift shop is downstairs off of the entrance hall," Wilson said. "But the woman came back up here just for a cup of tea?"

"And a slice of flapjack," Alyssa added. "It really is very good flapjack."

* * *

"Next stop, gift shop," Wilson said.

Raining laughed. "That rhymes."

To get to the gift shop, the children passed through the same galleries again, went down a flight of stairs, walked through four more galleries and then went down another flight of stairs to the entrance hall.

"You can't convince me that that woman walked all this way twice," Amal said. "No matter how delicious the flapjack is."

"And while carrying that fragile gift for her son," Wilson added. "It doesn't sound very likely."

One of the museum's volunteers – most of them residents from the nearby Floral Estates Retirement Homes – sat behind the gift-shop counter when they walked in.

"Hi, Mrs Malinofsky," Clementine said.

"Here's our resident artist," the elderly woman said with a smile. She got up from the stool she'd been sitting on. "They've stuck me in the gift shop today."

Clementine knew that many of the volunteers had very clear preferences about where they liked to work. Mrs Malinofsky liked the Greek and Roman exhibition. She loved answering questions. She'd once told Clementine she'd studied ancient art at university, in the 1950s. She'd been one of the first women to enrol at her college.

"Were you stuck here yesterday morning too?" Clementine asked.

"No," said Mrs Malinofksy as she walked around the counter. "Yesterday was Tuesday. I have a weekly appointment at the hair salon every Tuesday at nine o'clock."

"Do you know who was here yesterday morning then?" Wilson asked. "We want to ask them something."

"Let's see," said Mrs Malinofsky. She picked up a clipboard from the counter and ran her finger down the list of volunteers who'd signed in and out that week. "Ah, looks like it was that old grouch Mr Saunders."

"Do you know if he's volunteering in the museum today?" Wilson asked.

"Oh, he's here most days," Mrs Malinofsky said. "Mr Carbony would know where. He's in charge of all of the volunteers."

"Thanks a lot, Mrs Malinofsky," said Clementine.

"You kids wouldn't be nosing around

for any particular reason, would you?" Mrs Malinofsky asked. She gave them a pointed look over the top of her glasses. "Maybe investigating a certain theft?"

"We're staying out of trouble," Clementine promised.

"Because if you *are* investigating," the old woman went on, "I have a tip for you: that troublemaker Ruthie Rothchild was here all morning yesterday."

"Ruthie!" the four friends said together.

"Wait a minute," Amal said. "How do you know? You weren't here."

"Oh, we have a good natter after dinner at Floral Estates," Mrs Malinofsky said. "My friend Janice worked on the third floor. *She* saw that girl and her friends sniggering and whispering all over the museum."

CHAPTER 6
A new lead

"I don't remember seeing Ruthie while I was here," Clementine said. "Ugh. I don't want to see her. Are we going to have to see her?"

"One thing at a time," Amal said as the four friends crossed the entrance hall and headed towards Mr Carbony's office again. "We're investigating the lady with the box. She's our best lead."

"If we can track her down," Wilson pointed out. "She could be ten time zones away from here by now."

When the children stepped into Mr Carbony's office, he was on the phone with his back to the door. "Yes," he whispered. "I understand. It'll be fine. I have to go."

Mr Carbony turned to hang up the phone and saw the four children standing in the doorway. "Oh, hi!" he said, quickly bringing a big, bright smile to his face. "What can I do for you kids?"

"Who were you talking to just now?" Raining asked.

"What?" Mr Carbony said. "Oh, that? That was nothing. A personal call. You caught me! Making personal calls at work. Shame on me!" He laughed nervously.

"We wanted to ask you about one of the museum volunteers, Mr Carbony," Clementine said. "Mr Saunders. Is he working today?"

"Um, yes. I believe he's in the Dutch Masters exhibition this morning," said Mr Carbony as he spread his arms and shuffled the children back out of the office. "Now if you don't mind, I have a lot of work to do."

"One more thing," Wilson said, spinning and ducking under Mr Carbony's arm to face him. "The insurance payment. What's the name of the agent who signed it off?"

"Pardon?" Mr Carbony said. "What kind of question is that for an eight-year-old to ask?"

"I'm ten," Wilson said.

Mr Carbony sighed and rolled his eyes. "Preston," he told them. "I think his name was ... Gary Preston."

"Thanks," Wilson said. He ducked out of the door and closed it behind him. Then he turned to his friends. "You three find Saunders. Clementine, can I borrow your phone? I have some calls to make."

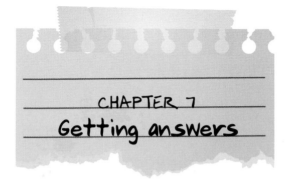

CHAPTER 7
Getting answers

Clementine, Amal and Raining left Wilson near the front desk and headed up to the second floor Dutch Masters Hall to find Mr Saunders.

"Is he going to be okay by himself?" Amal asked. Of the four friends, she was newest to Capitol City. She'd only known Wilson for a few months.

"Of course," Clementine said. "Wilson is one of the most capable people I know."

Raining grinned. "He takes care of me and Clementine more than we take care of him," he said with a chuckle.

The Dutch Masters exhibition took up nearly the whole back half of the museum's second floor. The hall displayed a collection of paintings by Rembrandt, Vermeer, Hals, Steen and several others who'd painted in the Netherlands in the seventeenth century.

When the three friends reached the top of the main staircase – wide-open and gleaming white, framed with panes of curved glass – they stopped and gasped. There, in plain sight, was Ruthie Rothchild, stalking around the gallery like a thief.

At least that's how Clementine saw her. Of course she didn't like Ruthie – at all.

And considering the fact that Clementine liked nearly everyone she'd ever met, that was saying something.

It wasn't that Clementine didn't have a reason. The two girls had known each other for nearly their entire lives, and Ruthie had been cruel to Clementine since day one. But thanks to her three new friends, Clementine was getting better at standing up for herself.

"I'll handle this," Clementine said. She strode up to Ruthie, who was crouching behind the white pillar holding up an ivory statue by Artus Quellinus, and cleared her throat loudly. "Ahem."

Ruthie turned and stood up straight, her eyebrows high, like she wasn't impressed at all. "What do you want?" she said.

"Why are you sneaking around up here?" Clementine asked. She tried to blow the hair that had fallen over her eyes out of her face, but it didn't work, and she just looked silly.

"Who are you, a security guard?" Ruthie snapped. "I can do what I want."

"Were you in the museum yesterday?" Clementine continued. She didn't usually do this type of questioning, but she was determined to get answers.

"Me?" Ruthie said with a smirk. "No, I was on Uranus."

Suddenly someone shouted from deeper in the gallery. "Owee ow oww!" came the deafening screech.

Clementine peered past the pedestal and saw Mr Saunders standing in the hall,

looking at the seat of the bench behind him and rubbing his bottom.

"Oh no!" Ruthie yelled. She gave Clementine a little shove. "You made me miss it. All that waiting and you ruined it for me."

"Ruined what?" Clementine asked.

"You idiot," Ruthie crossed her arms over her chest. It made her look *very* tough indeed. "I put a couple of pins on Old Man Saunders's favourite bench so I could watch him scream his head off when he sat on them. And you made me miss it."

"That's awful!" Clementine said, thinking she'd better go and see if Mr Saunders was all right.

"Yes, it is," said Ruthie. "You should be apologizing right now."

"Me?" Clementine said.

Ruthie rolled her eyes. "Yes, to *me*," she snapped. "Oh, never mind. You're wasting my time, and I want some lunch. See ya." She started to walk off towards the stairs, but then stopped and turned. "Oh, and nice job finally washing your face. It looked pretty silly with coloured pencil smeared all over it yesterday. My friends and I had a good laugh!"

With that, Ruthie shoved past Raining and Amal and went downstairs. They could hear her cackling the whole way.

CHAPTER 8
New evidence

"Mr Saunders?" Amal said as the three friends approached him slowly. Clementine had explained the trap Ruthie had set before they went over. She didn't want her friends wondering why the poor man was rubbing his bottom.

"Oh, hello," Mr Saunders said. Bending over, he pinched the tips of the pins, collecting them in the palm of his hand. He studied them carefully. "Dangerous litter, isn't it?"

"Yes," said Clementine.

"Did you kids have some questions about the gallery?" he asked.

"No, Mr Saunders," Clementine replied. "We wanted to ask you something about your shift yesterday."

"Yesterday?" he said, lowering his chin and looking down his nose.

"When the Gudea was stolen," Raining added.

"I see," Mr Saunders said. He sat down, remembering to check that the bench was clear of pins. "You're a gang of sleuths, are you?"

"Something like that," Amal said.

"The Statue of Gudea is one of my favourite pieces in the museum's collection," Clementine said. "I just really want them to get it back."

"Well, that makes two of us, then," Mr Saunders said. "Everyone else has got over-excited about Mr Carbony's new wing. The money's rolling in, they say."

"Yeah, we heard that too," Raining said.

"What would you like to know?" Mr Saunders asked.

Clementine told Mr Saunders about the woman in the Tea Room with the large package and her story about buying it in the gift shop that morning.

"Do you remember her?" Clementine asked. "You were working there yesterday, I think?"

"I was," Mr Saunders said, "but my shift didn't begin until just after ten o'clock. I missed my bus and decided to walk. As I'm a volunteer, I didn't think they'd be so cross about me being late. I don't recall selling anything that large to anyone during the time I was there."

"So who ran the shop when the museum opened at nine?" Amal asked, crossing her arms over her chest. "Someone had to be there."

"Mr Carbony," said Mr Saunders. "He was behind the till when I arrived. And let me tell you, he didn't look very pleased with me."

"Thanks, Mr Saunders," Clementine said. "You've been a big help."

The three friends turned to leave the exhibition. "Interesting how all roads seem to lead back to Mr Carbony, isn't it?" Amal said as they walked.

"Very interesting indeed," Raining agreed.

Clementine, Amal, and Raining ran into Wilson on the stairs back down to the entrance hall.

"Oh, good, I found you," Wilson said. "Just in time. Come down to the security office. Mr Preston from Global Property Insurance is here."

* * *

Moments later, the four friends gathered around Mr Preston in the security office. The

insurance agent sat in Judy's chair. She'd graciously given it up and stood off to the side, watching the interrogation and looking very amused.

"Thanks for coming down to talk to us, Mr Preston," Wilson said.

"Actually," Mr Preston said, "my office got a message that someone at the museum needed to meet me. I assumed I'd be seeing Mr Carbony about the recent theft."

"Speaking of the theft," Amal said, "can you tell us how the case was closed so quickly?"

"Do you four represent Mr Carbony?" Mr Preston asked.

"Um, yes," said Raining. "He sent us to speak to you. Isn't that right, Judy?"

The four friends looked at Judy. Mr Preston looked at Judy.

"That sounds about right to me," said Judy.

"Okay…" said Mr Preston, still not sounding quite sure. Clementine wondered what kind of an investigator would so readily believe four children. "But if you represent Mr Carbony, then you already know that he asked our office to move quickly so the museum could get the funds as soon as possible."

"So you moved quickly?" Clementine asked.

Mr Preston shrugged. "Well, yes," he said. "As far as I'm concerned, the statue is gone. If the police find it – well, then the museum will have to return the payment.

But these art thefts can take years to solve. These pieces often only resurface at a black-market auction, usually overseas."

"Thank you, Mr Preston," Wilson said. He put out his hand, and the man shook it, still looking very confused. "You've been very helpful. Judy will show you the way out."

Judy laughed and took Mr Preston's elbow as he stood up. "This way, sir," she said, leaving the four friends alone in the security office.

"This is really complicated," Wilson said, dropping into the big empty security chair. He pointed at the monitor in front of him. "There goes Mr Preston. He didn't do a very detailed investigation because..." – Wilson pointed at the monitor that showed

Mr Carbony's office – "… Mr Carbony asked him not to."

"Do you think they were in it together?" Amal asked.

Clementine gasped. "Do you think Mr Carbony stole the Gudea?" she said.

"But what about the woman in the Tea Shop?" Raining said. "It was obviously her!"

Wilson shook his head. "I don't think it was," he said. "I think she really did buy a gift and decided she wanted some tea afterwards."

"And a flapjack," Clementine added. "I can't say I blame her."

"So what do we do?" Amal said. "We don't have any proof."

"We go to Mr Carbony's office," Wilson said, leaning close to the monitor. "And we get some."

CHAPTER 9
Getting proof

"I don't understand," Clementine said as they stood in front of the closed door to Mr Carbony's office. "I thought we had already cleared Mr Carbony of the theft."

"He wasn't on the camera footage from the weekend," Raining pointed out.

"No one was," Amal added.

"That worried me too," Wilson admitted. "But then I realized that Mr

Carbony didn't *need* to come in over the weekend. If he hurried up to the third floor as soon as the museum opened, he could have snatched the statue after the motion-sensitive cameras were turned off."

"Why would he do it, though?" Clementine asked, slumping against the closed door. But the moment the words left her mouth, she knew. "The insurance money! He needed it for his new wing."

Suddenly Clementine was falling backwards into the office. Mr Carbony jumped to the side, and Clementine fell through the doorway and landed on the floor. "Ow!" she said, rubbing her hip.

"What are you four doing out here?" Mr Carbony said, obviously angry. "Were you listening at the door?"

"Would we have heard anything good?" Raining asked, grinning slyly.

Mr Carbony ignored him. "You four better explain yourselves, or I'll call Dr Wim down here to drag you out of this museum *for good*."

"I'll explain," Wilson said. "But first maybe you should call Dr Wim. She's going to need to listen to this too."

* * *

Dr Wim appeared moments later. "All right," she said, sitting on the sofa in Mr Carbony's office and crossing her legs. "I'm here. What do I need to listen to?"

Wilson explained to Dr Wim – with Mr Carbony listening closely as well – his theory of the crime. By the time he had finished, having implicated both Mr Carbony and Mr Preston in the theft, Dr Wim and Mr Carbony were nearly in tears – of laughter.

"Wilson," Dr Wim said, getting up from the sofa and putting a hand on Wilson's shoulder, "Mr Carbony didn't steal the Statue of Gudea."

"It surprised me too, Mum," Clementine said. "But it had to be him."

"That's right," Amal added. "Mr Preston told us that Mr Carbony asked him not to look in too much detail at the investigation so the insurance payout would come quickly. He obviously wanted to get his hands on the money for his new wing."

Mr Carbony's face flushed. He stammered and shuffled the papers on his desk.

"See?" Clementine said to her mum. "He can't even deny it!"

"But I do!" Mr Carbony hurried to say. "That is, I do deny *stealing* the Gudea." He opened his mouth to say something else, but seemed to think better of it and quickly looked down at his desk again.

"But?" Dr Wim said, standing up straight and crossing her arms.

"But..." Mr Carbony said, unable to look Dr Wim in the eye. "Well..." His face flushed, and he said, "I did ask Mr Preston to take the investigation lightly."

"How could you do that?" Dr Wim scolded, her eyebrows high and fierce.

"Look what we're about to accomplish!" Mr Carbony said, puffed up with pride. "The new wing – *my* new wing!"

"Oh, Mr Carbony," Dr Wim said, dropping onto the sofa and shaking her head. "This is insurance fraud."

"Is it?" Mr Carbony said as he dropped into his office chair. "I hadn't thought of that." He scratched his chin and twisted his mouth. Then he stared at the ceiling as if deep in thought.

Clementine noticed that Wilson had been looking more and more confused as the adults spoke. Finally he said, "Wait a minute. If Mr Carbony only meddled, but didn't actually *steal* the piece, then…"

The four friends looked at one another. Then they all turned back to Mr Carbony and exclaimed, "The gift shop!"

Mr Carbony nearly fell out of his chair. "What?"

Clementine stepped up to his desk. "You were working in the gift shop on Tuesday morning, weren't you?"

"Yes…" Mr Carbony said slowly. "Mr Saunders was late – again. Why do you want to know?"

"Did a woman come in and buy something" – Clementine roughly mapped out the size of the box with her hands – "about this big and have it boxed as a gift?"

"Yesterday morning?" Carbony asked. "No. A woman did come in, but she only asked for an old box I had behind the counter, so I gave it to her."

Clementine frowned and nodded slowly. "I think she needed that box," she said, "to hold the Gudea."

CHAPTER 10
Case solved?

Clementine thought it would probably be impossible to track down a random woman who'd visited the museum on Tuesday morning. But as luck would have it, a phone call to Alyssa up in the Tea Room was all it took.

"She used a credit card to pay," Alyssa told Clementine over the museum's internal phone. "I have her name, address and two telephone numbers right here."

The police tracked the mysterious woman down in no time at all. And just before closing time, the museum recieved a few unexpected guests.

Clementine, Raining, Wilson and Amal were all in the entrance hall with Dr Wim, about to leave for the day, when the big front doors burst open. In marched the oddest-looking group of people they'd ever seen.

Leading the group was a woman – short and slim, hunched over a little bit on long feet and with a pursed mouth and narrow nose that made her look a bit like a kangaroo rat. With her, or rather behind her, were three uniformed police officers and a man in a rumpled suit – Mr Preston.

"Hurry up! It's urgent," the woman at the front of the group shrieked.

"Look," said the police officer closest to her. Clementine noticed he had the woman by the elbow. Then she realized that *both* of the woman's hands were behind her back – and cuffed together. "This better not take long. I don't need the chief hearing about how you led us on a wild goose chase."

"It's no goose chase!" the woman snapped. "I'll show you right where it is. He told me to hide it here!" She strode across the hall, sneering at the four sleuths as she passed them.

"That must be her!" Clementine hissed at her friends. "The woman from the gift shop!"

"Why did they bring her here?" Raining said. "Did she want to steal something else?"

Mr Preston must have overheard them, because he came to a stop beside them and pulled off his hat. "Her name is Jacqueline Lecroix," he said. "And she claims there's a clue here that the police and I must see."

"A clue? That's impossible," Wilson said. "We went over the whole case – and solved it."

Clementine nodded. "We're sure it was her!" she said.

"The police are sure too," Mr Preston said. "They dusted for prints upstairs, and hers were a match for those found at the scene of the crime. There's one problem, though."

"What?" Clementine asked.

"She doesn't have the statue!" Mr Preston said. Then he hurried after the thief and her police escort.

CHAPTER 11
The real culprit

Clementine and her friends hurried after the group and caught up with them outside Mr Carbony's office.

"Open this door," Jacqueline Lecroix said as if *she* were in charge and the police had to do as she said.

"Wait just a minute!" Mr Carbony said as he rushed down the hall towards them, his bright orange tie fluttering behind him like a kite's tail. "That's my office!"

"Open it up," one of the police officers commanded. "This is part of a criminal investigation."

"I most certainly will not," Mr Carbony said. He stood in front of the office door with his arms folded across his chest as he panted for breath. "I know my rights!"

The officer held out a large blue envelope. "We have a warrant, sir," he said. "And Ms Lecroix says there's something we'll want to see inside."

Mr Carbony seemed to deflate almost instantly at that. "Oh," he said, taking the envelope. He stared at it, his eyes wide and his face pale. "It's not locked."

The officer opened the door, and

Jacqueline stepped in. As before, the little office was packed with boxes and crates. Clementine couldn't imagine how anyone could find anything in there.

"You'll have to uncuff me," Jacqueline said. She glared at Mr Carbony. "I'm sure he hid the statue somewhere in this mess."

"Can't do that," the officer said with a shake of his head. Instead, he pulled off his cap, rolled up his sleeves and started going through the boxes himself.

"What are you doing?" Carbony asked. "You don't *believe* this woman stashed her stolen goods in my office, do you?"

"Let's let the officer do his job, all right?" Dr Wim said, putting her hand on Mr Carbony's shoulder.

"Leave me alone," Mr Carbony

snapped, shaking her off. Finally seeming to realize there was nothing he could do, he flopped down in his desk chair and frowned.

* * *

The officer searched through Mr Carbony's boxes and crates for forty-five minutes before he found what he was looking for – a box about 30-centimetres wide by 60-centimetres high.

"That's it!" Jacqueline said, nodding madly. "That's the box! Open it!"

The officer picked up the letter opener from Mr Carbony's desk and slashed the packing tape across the top of the box. He opened the flaps and carefully reached inside. Packing peanuts fluttered out, drifting to the floor like snow, as the officer pulled out a small, stout statue of a man in a funny hat sitting with his hands folded together on his knees – the ancient Mesopotamian ruler himself, Gudea.

"I'm really confused," Wilson said. He sat on Mr Carbony's sofa with Dr Wim on one side and Mr Preston on the other.

Mr Preston stood up and put on his hat. "It seems like the hunch you kids had about Mr Carbony was right after all," he said. "He employed Ms Lecroix to steal the statue so he could collect the insurance money."

Dr Wim shook her head, looking devastated and disappointed. "So it's grand theft *and* insurance fraud."

"Theft?" Mr Carbony said as two police officers grabbed him by the elbows and pulled him up from his desk chair. "The statue hasn't even left the museum. It was in my office the whole time. And I am an employee of the museum, after all – there was no theft."

"We'll let the judge decide that," said the police officer. "You and Ms Lecroix can explain everything – *in court*."

CHAPTER 12
A happy ending

At home later that evening, Clementine curled up on the sofa with her mother to listen to the classical music station while they both sipped herbal tea.

"Do you think Mr Carbony will really get away with it?" Clementine asked. "I mean, was all that stuff he said about it not being theft because the Gudea never even left the building true?"

"Not a chance," her mum said. "And even if he did somehow manage to convince a judge of that, we've got him on insurance fraud and conspiracy for sure."

Clementine nodded firmly. "Good," she said. "That's good." She sighed heavily.

"Is something else the matter, Clementine?" her mother asked.

"I'm glad we caught him and that wicked lady, but I feel bad, too," Clementine said. "I mean, I'm obviously glad the Gudea is back, but now the museum will have to return all that insurance money."

"True," said Dr Wim.

"Which means no new wing for the museum," Clementine said sadly.

"Oh, I wouldn't worry about that," Dr Wim said. A mischievous smile spread across her lips. "It seems that Mr Carbony's pleas to the public this morning were so effective that we'll be able to build the new wing even without the insurance money. And it would be in very poor taste for any of the donors to withdraw their offers at this point, I think. Isn't that wonderful?"

Clementine smiled as she remembered Mr Carbony's speech from that morning. "Then I suppose that this silver lining has no grey cloud after all."

Steve B.

About the Author

Steve Brezenoff is the author of more than fifty middle-school chapter books, including the Field Trip Mysteries series, the Ravens Pass series of thrillers and the Return to Titanic series. In his spare time, he enjoys video games, cycling and cooking. Steve lives in Minnesota, USA, with his wife, Beth, and their son and daughter.

Lisa W.

About the Illustrator

Lisa K. Weber is an illustrator currently living in California, USA. She graduated from Parsons School of Design in 2000 and then began freelancing. Since then, she has completed many print, animation and design projects, including graphic novelizations of classic literature, character and background designs for children's cartoons and textiles for dog clothing.

GLOSSARY

curator person in charge of a museum; they will often decide which pieces to collect and display in the museum

easel angled stand or frame that holds an artist's canvas

fragile very easily broken or damaged

gallery room or building for displaying works of art

implicate suggest that someone was involved in something, like a crime

interrogation questioning of someone to discover hidden facts, usually about a crime

intruder someone who enters a place without permission

investigate search in detail, to search for information about something

precaution something you do ahead of time in order to make sure things work out well or to make sure nothing bad happens

sleuth someone who solves mysteries or is good at finding out facts

DISCUSSION QUESTIONS

1. Have you ever been to an art gallery? Talk about what it was like. Did you have a favourite piece of art or a least favourite?

2. Do you think that the museum will raise enough money to build the educational wing? Discuss why or why not.

3. Which artistic activity do you like best: painting, drawing, sculpting or something else? Talk about why you like it.

WRITING PROMPTS

1. A lot of people were upset when the Statue of Gudea was stolen. Write about an object you have lost that was important to you. Why was it important? Did you find it?

2. Clementine likes to go to different exhibitions at the Capitol City Museum of Art in her spare time. Write about what you like to do during your spare time.

3. The Capitol City Museum of Art depends on volunteers to do things such as running the gift shop and answering questions about the exhibitions. Imagine you could volunteer at any museum. Write a paragraph about what you'd like to do there.

ART INFORMATION

The Tate holds the national collection of British art from 1500 to the present day. It was founded in 1897 by Henry Tate and its collection now includes over 70,000 artworks by over 3,000 artists from all over the world. The Tate is made up of four museums; Tate Britain, Tate Modern (both located in London), Tate Liverpool and Tate St Ives. The Tate also hosts the Turner Prize, an annual prize presented to a British artist under the age of 50.

Famous Artists

Barbara Hepworth (1903 – 1975) was a British artist and sculptor best known for her modernist sculptures. The Barbara Hepworth Museum and Sculpture Garden in St Ives, Cornwall, preserves the artist's studio and garden much as they were while she lived and worked there.

Damien Hirst (1965 – present) is a British artist well known for his series of artworks featuring dead animals. One of his most famous pieces, *Impossibility of Death in the Mind of Someone Living*, features a tiger shark immersed in a vat of formaldehyde.

David Hockney (1937 – present) is a British artist influenced by popular culture. He was an important contributor to the pop art movement in the 1960s and is well known for his portraits, landscapes and still lifes (some of which he now paints on his iPad). Hockney is also a well-regarded stage designer and has designed sets and costumes for operas and ballets around the world.

Edward Hopper (1882 – 1967) was an American painter. He often painted realistic scenes of everyday life but focused on themes of loneliness. His most famous painting, *Nighthawks*, shows people sitting in a restaurant late at night.

Georgia O'Keeffe (1887 – 1986) was an influential American painter who liked to paint nature. She is best known for very close-up paintings of flowers and desert landscapes of the south-western United States.